FRANKLY FRANNIE

Check, Please!

by AJ Stern • illustrated by Doreen Mulryan Marts

SCHOLASTIC INC.
New York Toronto London Auckland
Sydney Mexico City New Delhi Hong Kong

For Puggy, my grandmother,
who always takes me to fancy restaurants!—AJS

Thanks as always to everyone at Penguin: Francesco
Sedita, Bonnie Bader, Caroline Sun, Christine
Duplessis, Scottie Bowditch, Kimberly Lauber,
Jordan Hamessley, Meagan Bennett, and my editor,
Judy Goldschmidt. Your support and enthusiasm
is unparalleled! To Julie Barer, of course, and her
assistant, William Boggess. To my family and friends
for their support.—AJS

No part of this publication may be reproduced, stored in a retrieval system,
or transmitted in any form or by any means, electronic, mechanical,
photocopying, recording, or otherwise, without written permission of the
publisher. For information regarding permission, write to Grosset & Dunlap,
a division of Penguin Young Readers Group, a member of Penguin Group (USA) Inc.,
345 Hudson Street, New York, NY 10014.

ISBN 978-0-545-33277-4

Text copyright © 2010 by AJ Stern.
Illustrations copyright © 2010 by Doreen Mulryan Marts.
All rights reserved. Published by Scholastic Inc.,
557 Broadway, New York, NY 10012, by arrangement with
Grosset & Dunlap, a division of Penguin Young Readers Group,
a member of Penguin Group (USA) Inc. SCHOLASTIC and associated
logos are trademarks and/or registered trademarks of Scholastic Inc.

12 11 10 9 8 7 6 5 4 3 2   11 12 13 14 15 16/0

Printed in the U.S.A.   40

First Scholastic printing, January 2011

CHAPTER

1

It is a scientific fact that my school fair happens once a year. I wish it happened **twentyteen** times a year, but my dad says "You can't have it all," and that is not an opinion.

The reason my school fair is so fantastical is that they let **all** the students work there! And if you don't already know this about me, I'm a **really** jobbish kind of person. A for instance of what I mean is that I would like a job with an office.

The job at the school fair is not in an office. It's in the cafeteria, but that's okay because it's still a job. The job is called *Spaghetti Lunch*. Spaghetti Lunch is where volunteers from Chester High School make spaghetti and the middle-school kids serve it. I am in elementary school, so my job is to pass out bread and water. That's certainly a good job because the water comes in a professional-looking pitcher and the bread comes in an official-looking basket.

The morning of the fair, my best friend Elliott and I were so excitified, we could hardly sit still in the back of the car. My mom looked at us in the rearview mirror and smiled.

"You're like a couple of monkeys back there," she teased. "What are you so happy about?" she asked.

"Spaghetti Lunch," I sang.

"And Grab Bag," Elliott added. I nodded, because I agreed with this. **Grab Bag** is where you reach your hand into a big bag that is filled with foreverteen prizes. When you pull out your prize, you are so **excited** because you don't know what's coming.

The moment you see the prize you grabbed is the exact moment you remember that you've always wanted that prize! A for instance of what I mean is that one year I grabbed **candy lipstick**. It wasn't until after I pulled it out that I remembered I had always wanted candy lipstick! You always feel lucky at Grab Bag, and that is not an opinion.

"I'm excited for the raffle this year," my mom told us as she drove into the school parking lot. A raffle is where someone pulls out a name from a jug. Whoever's name is chosen **wins the prize**. "They're raffling off a free dinner at the new restaurant, Balloo," my mom continued. Elliott and I were not so interested in this prize. We were interested in getting to the fair, which is why my mom dropped us off **exactly** in front of the school doors before she looked for a parking space.

"I hope they don't close the raffle before I get there," she said as Elliott and I jumped out of the car. Then my mom leaned over toward the passenger side window and called after me. "Now behave yourself, Mrs. Miller," she said, making one eyebrow go up a step.

"I will!" I yelled as Elliott and I ran up the school stairs and pulled open the front doors. We were so **overwhelmified** by what we saw, our faces almost fell off our heads. There were tables set up with lemonade and face paint and books and games and prizes and a foreverteen amount of things to do. I wanted to do **all of them** at the exact same time.

"Last call for the raffle," my sort-of friend Millicent's mom called out. Millicent is only my sort-of friend because she likes to read books more than she likes to talk to real, live people, like me. Her mother is the head of the Parents' Association, which is why she's in charge of the **raffle**. "Last call before we close!"

I tugged on Elliott's hand. "Come

on. We have to write my mom's name down," I told him.

Elliott and I went over to the raffle table and found the big jug that read: DINNER AT BALLOO. I did not understand why the restaurant was not called *Balloon*. Maybe they ran out of *n*'s? Then I saw that the raffle cost one dollar and we had exactly **no dollars**! That is when I got an idea. I walked over to Millicent's mom and said, "Excuse me." Sometimes I get embarrassed to "Mr." or "Mrs." someone.

Millicent's mom looked down at me and said, "Hi, Frannie! Do you need me?"

"Well . . . Elliott and I don't have any money. We were wondering if we could make you an IOU for exactly one dollar," I asked her. "And when my mom comes, we can give it to you?"

"That's a great idea, Frannie," she said. I was very **proud** of my great idea. My dad is the one who gave me the idea about IOUs. They're really special because if you say the letters out loud they sound like the words: *I. OWE. YOU.* Sometimes my dad writes them for me if he has to miss my bedtime because of work. They go like this: *IOU one extra-long good-night story!*

Since Elliott's handwriting is very **perfect**, I had him write the IOU and my mom's name on the raffle card. Then I handed Millicent's mom the **IOU**, folded up the card, and dropped her name inside the big jug.

Our job wasn't starting yet, so we decided we would go from table to table until it was ten minutes later.

We guessed how many jelly beans

were in a cookie jar. I guessed **421** and Elliott guessed **422**. We had our fortunes told. Elliott is going to be a fireman and I'm going to work in a real office! *And* I'm going to have an **assistant**, which is the exact thing I want for Christmas!

Finally, it was exactly **noon o'clock** and Elliott and I went downstairs to start our job. I secretly hoped we would get to wear **uniforms**. Uniforms are very extremely grown-up.

CHAPTER

You will not believe what our class got to wear for Spaghetti Lunch. **Aprons!** And they weren't the baby kind that you have to tie behind your back AND your neck. They were the kind you just tie around your waist.

Elliott's babysitter, Tenley, was the boss of Spaghetti Lunch. She was volunteering with her friends from Chester High. Tenley is very serious about food. She thinks being healthy is very important and she really hates sugar, which is something I never knew a person could hate. But she is very nice, *and* she is in twelfth grade, which is the oldest grade of all. She waved when she saw us, in front of the entire school! Because she was the boss of Spaghetti Lunch AND in twelfth grade, we felt twicely important.

Our teacher, Mrs. Pellington, stood with Tenley at a table next to the kitchen door and clapped to get our attention. Then she explained how to do our jobs, exactly.

"No table should be empty. A good waiter or waitress makes sure every table has bread and water on it."

That was when Tenley made an *I just remembered something I need to tell everyone* face.

"Also, a good waiter or waitress always washes their hands before the beginning of food service, so if anyone hasn't done so yet, now would be the time," she announced. It is a scientific fact that germs are not healthy, which is why Tenley is very serious about clean hands.

A few kids went into the kitchen to use the sink, but not me and Elliott. When Tenley saw us headed in that direction, she took out her wipes and gave one to each of us. That was the third way she made us feel important!

"Remember," Mrs. P. told us when everyone came back from washing their hands, "when you see someone coming with a plate of spaghetti, move out of the way. The plates are very hot. Plus, we don't want anyone to trip and spill spaghetti **all over the place**. And under no circumstance are you to serve anything but bread and water. Is that understood?" Mrs. P. asked us. We nodded our heads.

"Frannie?" she asked me.

I quickly turned my head away from Tenley, who was blobbing **slippy piles of spaghetti** onto the plates.

"Do *you* understand?" Mrs. P. asked in a voice that said *you'd better understand.*

I looked Mrs. P. right in her eyeballs and nodded. This told her I was paying **strict** attention.

"It is a scientific fact that I understand," I told her. And that is when the first customer came into the cafeteria! Soon there was another customer, and then another, until there were a machillion of them. And they all looked very hungry. I brought water and bread to **every** single table. Sometimes the customers were parents and other times they were teachers. I got so good at my job that I even offered to pour the water for my customers. Only one customer said yes, but then she changed her mind when I lifted the pitcher and my hand started to **wobble**.

Soon everyone had their bread and water and things got **boring**. Our job now was to wait. Even though I am a good waiter, I am not good at waiting. Elliott and I waited together, but even then I felt really fidgety. That is why I decided to walk around and see if everyone had all the bread and water that they would ever need in their entire lives.

Over in the corner, I saw a really **teenaged** girl customer sitting by herself waiting for spaghetti. I knew she was waiting because she kept looking at the kitchen with a *where is my spaghetti??* face.

She was looking all around like she was trying to get someone's attention. Then she caught my eye and pointed behind me. I turned to look but didn't see what she was pointing at. When I turned back she was pointing **even harder**, if you can believe that. I turned around again and, behind the older kids, I saw waiting plates of spaghetti. OH! She wanted me to get her a plate of spaghetti!

I felt so much pride-itity that she chose me to be her waitress. I walked over to the counter where all the plates of spaghetti were sitting and I saw the exact **perfect** one. The plate was almost overflowing with spaghetti and steam was floating off the top. For a hungry customer, this was certainly the best choice. I walked right up to it and because I am **really smart** about when to use one hand or two, I picked the plate up with both hands. It was only when I turned around and took some steps toward the teenaged girl that I noticed a really bad feeling on my hands. And less than a centimeter of a second later I realized what the bad feeling was. The plate was boiling-its-head-off hot. I was too **shocktified** to move, but I had to do something with the plate.

Mrs. P. was rushing over to me, and right behind her, I saw my mom.

I don't know how she ended up in exactly the part of the cafeteria where I was doing **a bad thing**. I hadn't even seen her come into school when she was finished parking the car.

Before I even knew what in the whole wide world of America was happening, the very hot plate **flung** out of my hands. Then, like it was in slow motion, I watched the tomato-sauced spaghetti fly across the air and plop in a **splat** all over Mrs. P.'s nice white shoes and the bottom of her white pants.

"Frannie!" my mom shouted, crashing her palm against her forehead.

That is when the entire world stopped breathing and the whole cafeteria, including the really teenaged girl, turned to stare at me.

My face turned tomato sauce red.
Mrs. P. was staring at her feet. It was
horrendimous. I have never been so
humilified in my whole life, and that is
not an opinion.

"I . . . I . . . The plate was very hot," I
tried to explain.

"That's exactly why you were not
supposed to touch it!" Mrs. P. said,
raising her voice a little bit.

"I'm sorry, Mrs. P.," I told her. "I'll
help you clean up."

"I think you've done enough already,
Frannie," Mrs. P. said in her *you stay
right where you are, young lady* voice.

My mom was already on the floor
with some paper towels and Tenley
came rushing out with **a mop**. I did
not even want to turn and see what
Elliott's expression looked like.

"Mrs. P., I am so sorry," my mom said. "I insist that you send me the bill for the cleaning."

"Oh, that's okay," Mrs. P. told her. "I never wear my good things to school, anyway."

"Nevertheless," my mom began (*nevertheless* is a really grown-up word I have to remember to use more oftenly), "why don't you go wash up and I'll take over for you."

"You wouldn't mind?"

"Of course not. It's the least I can do."

Then Mrs. P. turned to me and said, "Frannie, I'm afraid that I'm going to have to ask you to sit out the rest of Spaghetti Lunch." That is when my mouth almost fell down to my own shoes. I looked at my mom.

"That's a very lenient punishment,

Frannie," my mom explained.
Lenient meant "that's not a very
bad punishment at all!" I knew the
word *lenient* from the last time I was
punished, which was exactly not so
long ago.

Mrs. P. pointed to a very strict
chair in the most **boring** section of the
cafeteria. It was all the way off in the
corner where nothing ever happened!

"And I'd like you to think about
the difference between good helping
and bad helping. Is that clear?"

I nodded my head yes.

"Okay, Mrs. P.," I said. "I'm
sorry about your shoes and pants. I
really am. I will go think about some
differences now in the boring area."
And that is when I **slunked** my way
over to the bad section. I sat there for

three months and forty hundred years.
Mrs. P. came back from the bathroom
all cleaned up, but with spaghetti
stains. Then she clapped **twice** to get
our attention.

"Okay, class, let's line up and
take a bow, because we did such a
great job!"

I love bows! I jumped right out
of my **boring seat** and ran over to
stand next to Elliott. And that is when
the second most horrendimous thing
happened. Mrs. P. turned to me and
said in a really strict way, "Frannie,
please go back to your seat. I'll tell
you when it's time to get up."

I could not in a millionteen years
believe this! Elliott's mouth almost
fell off his face at the same time as
mine. I was shocktified. I did not

know that punishments were **more important than bows**.

I slunked back to my chair and watched my entire class take a really important bow **without me**. I could tell that Elliott was upset that I wasn't next to him. I knew because he didn't bow as hard as I've seen him bow in the past. The whole world of the cafeteria clapped for the good job my class did. I love getting claps, but I didn't do a good job, so I didn't get any. I was very angrified at myself for spilling **hot spaghetti** all over Mrs. P.'s clothes. I was never going to touch a hot plate ever again. Not in a machillion years.

CHAPTER

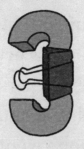

My mom was still upset with me when it was time for the **raffle**. She was a really fancy kind of mad: She was cross. Cross is worse than angry because I don't really know what it means.

We settled into our seats in the auditorium and Elliott and I jittered our legs with excitement. I felt my belly fill up with **moths and butterflies**. Even though I was being crossed at, I still wanted my mom to win the raffle.

She didn't know that Elliott and I put her name in the big jug. She also didn't know we owed Millicent's mom **one dollar**, but I would tell her later. If she won then she'd be less grumpy and maybe she'd uncross herself at me.

There was a lot of chattering, and then soon everyone went really quiet. Millicent's mom came on the stage carrying a big jug with millions of papers stuffed inside it. Millicent stood next to her. For once her head was not in a book. Maybe Millicent loves her mom more than she loves books.

Then, before the big raffle for the families, Millicent's mom held up the **jelly bean jar** that we guessed at.

"We had a lot of very fine guesses, but no one guessed the exact number," she told us. That sentence got a big groan. "There are 409 jelly beans in here. The person with the closest guess was only twelve jelly beans off. At 421, our winner is Frannie B. Miller! Frannie, please come to the stage and collect your prize!"

It is a scientific fact that I have never won anything before. I was so **nervous** to go up on the stage alone that I grabbed Elliott's hand and made him come with me.

"Congratulations," Millicent's mom said into the **microphone** as she handed me the extremely heavy jar.

"Thank you for your congratulations," I said back into the microphone. Then added, "Elliott guessed 422, so I'm going to share this with him." And that was when the crowd applauded, **actually**.

Can you even believe that fact? Not only was I the winner of 409 jelly beans, but I was **the winner** of clapping! It certainly made up for losing out on Spaghetti Lunch clapping!

Then Millicent's mom announced that it was time for the big dinner raffle and Elliott and I went back to our seats. She made it sound like getting to eat at the Balloon restaurant was the **best** part of the entire raffle, but it's a scientific fact that it was not.

Someone in the audience made a **drumroll** sound. Millicent's mom stuck her hand in the jug. After feeling around for nearly fifty hours, she pulled out a piece of paper.

And you'll never believe what I'm about to tell you: *That* piece of paper she pulled out looked EXACTLY like the white piece of paper Elliott wrote my mom's name on. It took her thirty-seven hours to unfold the piece of paper and a century before she read it out loud.

"Well, what do you know!" she said in a *what a coincidence!* voice. "The winner of the dinner raffle is none other than Anna Miller, Frannie Miller's mother!" Everyone in the audience clapped. I looked over at my mom, whose face was bright red and twisted in a confusified expression. And that's when I gave her my big *that's right, I entered you in the raffle while you were trying to find a parking space* smile. She gave me a very big smile back and grabbed my hand. "That was a very thoughtful thing to do, Bear," she whispered in my ear as she led me back to the stage.

That was when my **heart** almost exploded out of my own chest.

Onstage, my mother collected the gift certificate and then said thank you into the microphone and we went back to our seats. Then she whispered to me, "It's a *French* restaurant!"

Two seconds before I didn't even care about eating at

a fancy restaurant, but now I couldn't wait. That was when I squeezed my mom's hand, which told her in no words how excitified I was, nevertheless.

CHAPTER 4

That night at dinner I showed my dad the big jar with my half of the **jelly beans**. Showing my dad was one of the hugest mistakes of my career because he acted just like he did with Halloween candy. I was allowed to **scoop** out one handful and then he'd hold on to the rest until I was allowed another scoop. It is a scientific fact that I planned on **scooping** out the best handful of jelly beans ever, and that is not an opinion. Plus, I was also going to hide beans all around the house so that they would last forever.

After my dad put the jelly bean jar away, me and my mom told him all about the fair, my IOU (which my mom paid back), and even the part about the **spaghetti** on Mrs. P.'s shoes.

"But I already got in trouble about that," I told him, in case he wanted to punish me about it all over again.

"Did you get a fair punishment?" he asked.

"Yes!" I said, and very quickly changed the subject before he and my mom had a chance to send **brain messages** to each other that my punishment really *was* too lenient.

"And Mom won a raffle!"

My dad looked at her and she gave him the hugest smile.

"You'll never guess what it was," she said.

"A new car?" Dad asked.

"Nope," Mom answered.

Dad tried again. "A new house?"

"Nope," Mom said.

"Fourteen billion dollars?" he tried one last time.

Then Mom leaned in, put her hand on his, and said, "Dinner at Balloo." It is a scientific fact that dinner at Balloon is not better than **fourteen billion dollars**, but the way my mom said it made it seem like it was.

"Well, I'll be!" my dad said, slapping his hand down on the table.

"The chef is supposed to be amazing," my mom told him. "But I haven't seen a word about it from any of the food critics."

"It might be too early for them to send a food critic," my dad said.

What in the worldwide of America were they talking about?

"What's a food critic?" I asked.

"A food critic is someone who eats at restaurants and writes about the food and the service."

"Is this a real, live, actual job?" I asked.

"Yes, it is," my mom told me.

"Do food critics have offices?"

My parents looked at each other with **question mark faces**.

"I think they probably write in an office, yes," my mom said.

In my entire life as a person, I had never heard about people eating for their actual job. Being a food critic sounded like the most **spectacular job** in the worldwide of America.

It was very easy to picture myself as a food critic. I saw myself sitting alone, in the middle of a long, **rectangular** table, while waiters put one plate of food after another in front of me. The customers were all turned to face me, like an audience at the theater, and everyone was very quiet while I chewed. After every bite, I announced to the restaurant what I thought about the food, and all the eaters would **ooh** and **ahhh** and maybe even clap.

But then I was a little stumpified.

"But how do you describe the taste of food?"

"Well, take this soup for example.

Why don't we all have a sip and describe the taste to one another?" my mother suggested.

My dad, mom, and I scooped up a big spoonful of the most **delicious** vegetable soup that my dad made.

My mom said, "This soup is comforting and reminds me of sitting in front of the fireplace with my two favorite people."

My dad said, "To me the soup tastes light and airy, not too watery, salty but flavorful, and it hits the spot."

And then I said, "It tastes like carrots, celery, zucchini, and clear broth." I looked down at the soup to make sure I wasn't leaving anything out, and then quickly added, "And rice!"

My parents smiled because they knew I was **exactly right**.

"Good job, Frannie," my dad said, and I smiled from one side of our house to the other. I *loved loved loved* when my dad Good-Job-Frannie'd me.

I took another sip and they looked at me and waited. It was just like I imagined it would be at the restaurant where I was working as a **food critic**. I swished it around in my mouth and chewed on all the vegetables, swallowed, and then looked up at the ceiling until I had the **perfect** description.

"The taste I taste is a soupy taste," I told them with a very professional voice.

"That's a good start, Bird," my dad said.

My dad is the only person who calls me that. It is a scientific fact that **Bird** is my middle name, but please do not tell anyone.

"Vegetable soupy," I added.

When I saw the pride-itity on my dad's face after I said *vegetable soupy*, I knew right then and there I was meant to be a food critic.

CHAPTER 5

After school the next day, my mom and I were sitting on the living room floor making a **scrapbook** together. We were very concentratey, which

is why we both did shoulder jumps when my dad came through the front door.

"I have some very interesting news!" my dad said as he put down his briefcase.

"What? Tell us!" my mom said.

"Maria Cross *might* be going to Balloo the same night we're going!" he said. And then before I could even ask the question out loud, he turned to me and answered it: "She's the food critic at the *Chester Times*!"

This was a for instance of when my brain thinks two things at the exact same time. The first thought was: *If Cross were my last name, I would make sure everyone in the entire world knew it was a* last name *kind of cross, not an* I'm mad at you *kind of cross.*

The **second brain thought** made me stand up and ask out loud, "Food critics are famous?!"

"Some are, yes," said my dad. "But Maria Cross is the *most* famous. In Chester, at least."

"How do you know where Maria Cross is going to be?" my mom asked.

"Well, I was in line at the grocery store when the woman behind me took a call. She was whispering, as if she didn't want anyone to hear, but she was *right* behind me, so it was hard *not* to. Anyway, I heard her say something like, 'Maria's going to Balloo either this Friday or next.'"

My mom **scrunched** her face and thought about this for a second.

"How do you know the woman on the phone was talking about Maria

Cross? Couldn't she have been talking about a different Maria?"

"Good question," said my dad. I could tell that whatever he was about to say actually filled him with **pride-itity**. "I know because the woman mentioned Maria's newspaper the very next time she spoke. She said something like, 'That's how they do it at the *Chester Times* . . .'"

I looked at my mom to see if she was **convinced**.

"Hunhhh . . .," she said, which meant that she was! (I'm very smart about whether my mom is convinced.)

"Wow. Can we get there early for a front-row seat?" I asked.

Now my parents scrunched their faces at *me*!

"Front-row seat? We're going to a restaurant, Birdy, not the theater," said my dad. "Plus, she also might *not* be going this Friday night, when we're going. She might be going *next* Friday."

They certainly didn't know as much about restaurants as I thought they did.

"But we still have to be up close so we can hear what she says," I explained. "Then we'll know what's good and bad and order all the right things!"

My parents were silent for exactly one-half of a second before they both laughed out loud.

"That's not exactly how it works," my mom said, once she stopped laughing.

I sat back down, disappointed.

"Well then, how *does* it work?" I asked.

"First of all, the restaurants aren't

supposed to know that the critic is there because the critic doesn't want **special** service," she said.

"Why not?" This **confused** me. I didn't know anyone who didn't like special service.

"Because a critic's job is to tell people what to expect when they visit a restaurant. But if the chef puts more care into preparing the critic's food, then the food described by the critic isn't the same food everyone else gets to eat," my mom explained.

I thought about that for a second until my brain decided it **made sense**.

"So how does it work, exactly? If no one knows the famous food person is there, then how does the famous food person get any food?" I asked.

"The critic makes a reservation,

just like everyone else. They get their own table and when they get the menu, the fun part begins," my dad explained, adding, "The critic orders as much food on the menu as possible without looking like too much of a pig."

"Sometimes they bring friends so it doesn't look weird that one person is ordering everything on the menu," my mom said.

My dad leaned back. "Then, when they're done, they write an article about everything they experienced. And then the newspaper publishes it."

That is when I got the most spectacular idea. "Can we invite Elliott to Balloon?" I asked.

My parents looked at each other. Sometimes this means they are having brain conversations.

"Sure we can," my dad said.

"We'll write a review, too."

"What a great idea, Frannie!"

"Which newspaper does Maria Cross put her articles in again?"

"The *Chester Times* of New York."

"Oh! That's *my* newspaper! Remember when I had my picture taken with the new mayor of Chester and it was published in that exact newspaper?" I reminded them.

Since the *Chester Times* already knew who I was, there was a good chance they'd put something I wrote in their paper. Right then I knew I had better write a review I could be proud of.

CHAPTER
6

I did not know it was possible to be **nervous** about going to a restaurant, but standing outside Balloon on Friday night, I noticed how many moths and **butterflies** were swimming around my belly. My parents and Elliott were excitified to go inside, but I asked them to wait. I had to check inside my briefcase to make sure that everything I had packed was still there: my résumé (which is a list of all the jobs I've had), my business cards, two pads of stapled-together scrap paper, two pencils, my dad's old pair of glasses with the lenses taken out (he wears contacts now), and an envelope.

I closed my briefcase and nodded to my parents and Elliott to let them know that I was ready. Then we went inside, and you would not even **believe** what we saw. First of all, there were a hundredteen people eating dinner. It was the most crowded restaurant I had ever seen. There were even people standing in the front part of the restaurant waiting to get a table. Music was playing and there was **clatter** from all the silverware and china and the sound of a hundredteen people talking to one another.

How in the worldwide of America

was I supposed to review all this? I didn't think I knew enough words to describe any of it. That's when I got a geniusal **idea**. I turned to Elliott.

"Do you want to describe the restaurant and I'll describe the food?"

Elliott's eyeballs almost popped out of his head.

"Yes!" he said.

"Okay. When we get to our table, I'll give you some paper and a pencil."

I could tell that Elliott was very **happy** I asked him. His face was filled with pride-itity.

When we sat down, I tried to see if there was a lady sitting all by herself who could be Maria Cross, but I didn't see anyone alone. Maybe she wasn't there yet.

One **centimeter** of a second after

we sat down, a waiter in an actual tuxedo came over and gave us the hugest menus I'd ever seen. They were so **heavy** that Elliott and I each had to hold up ours with both of our hands. We were stumpified by the menus. A for instance of what I mean is that the words on the menu were not even in English. They were in French!

Another for instance of why the menu was so **confusifying** was that it didn't have any pictures of what the food looked like. I like seeing **pictures** of the food because if it looks delicious then that's what I point to when the waiter comes over. I also like it when the picture has a number underneath because all you have to remember is the number and not some long, complicated food name.

Like *tortelnoodi* or *spaghettivealinaise*.

Before my mom had a chance to translate the words for me and Elliott, the tuxedo waiter came over, and when he asked if we'd like to hear the specials, my parents said yes.

This was not such a good idea. The waiter bent down so he was closer to our **eardrums** and turned his face channel to very serious. Then he started to tell us about all the different dishes in a very **whispery**, storytelling voice. He went on and on about each little thing in the dish and I thought he might cry. It was like he was talking about his favorite aunt whom he loved so much, but couldn't see because she lived **far, far, far away in Pennsylvania**.

He told us how everything was

cooked and what everything came with and sometimes he **fluttered** his hands like he was pretend-cooking. Other times he kissed his fingertips and then tossed them up in the air like he was throwing a real, live **kiss** across the room! His accent was already funny, but sometimes he danced the words around when he said them, or stretched them out. Like, instead of saying *little*, he said *leeeeetle*. The worst of it was that he did not stop talking, ever.

Elliott and I couldn't even help ourselves. We were trying not to be obvious about laughing, but our laughing kept making our menus bounce up and down. I tried very hard to think of terrible things so I would **stop laughing**, but it didn't work.

Remember how sad it was when your whole class took a bow at Spaghetti Lunch and you had to sit all by yourself and watch? But even that didn't help me. It made it worse, actually.

Soon, **tears ran down my face**, and my shoulders were shaking up and down at how the serious waiter didn't even know how funny he was. How could my parents keep such straight faces? I looked over at my dad, whose lips turned up at the ends into the teeniest, tiniest **curl smile** (I'm very smart about curl smiles), which is how I knew that he was trying not to laugh. And my mom scrunched her eyes to show she was being very **concentratey**, but I know that she was also trying not to laugh.

Then my dad said, "Thank you. I think we'll need another minute."

When the waiter walked away, Elliott and I dropped our menus, but, instead of **bursting out laughing**, we just sort of . . . stopped. My parents looked at us, both with strict faces.

"What?" I asked with very wide eyes, like I didn't know what I did wrong.

"You know better than to laugh at people," my mom said, being a little bit **scoldish**.

"We weren't laughing at *him*!" I told her. "We were laughing at the way he was talking!"

"That's the same thing. Plus, he was just trying to do his job and you made him feel bad."

I hung my head down.

"Oh," I said. I hadn't meant to make anyone feel bad. It's just that he was saying all these fancy words in a very serious and **emergency type of way** and it tickled me from the inside, and when you are tickled from the inside, you don't have a choice about laughing. You just HAVE to.

"Sorry," I told her.

"Sorry," Elliott added. I could tell he felt bad, too, because he had worry on his forehead. That's when his forehead gets lots of lines on it from too much **worrying**.

"Good. Now you can apologize to him when he returns."

My Cheerio eyes practically zoomed out of my head.

"*To* him? But he's a stranger!"

"Yes, but you're with us, so it's okay to talk to him," my mom explained.

"Strangers have feelings, too," my dad added.

He was right about that, too, and that gave me a very **bad-day feeling** in my belly. I hated hurting people's feelings, especially grown-up men who were very **serious** about restaurant specials.

When he came back to the table, I looked up at the waiter to apologize. "I'm sorry that we laughed," I said, looking at his eyebrows instead of his **eyeballs** so I wouldn't feel so ashamed.

"I'm sorry, too," Elliott added.

The waiter made a little laugh and said, "You are not the only children who have laughed at my accent."

Even though he gave a little laugh, he did not look happy about this fact.

"I will tell all the children of the world to stop it," I told him in a very serious tone.

"Thank you, mademoiselle," said the waiter, and then he **flipped** open his waiter pad. We gave our orders, and when I was done ordering my spaghetti from the kids' section of the menu, I got up all my bravery to ask the waiter a very important question.

"Excuse me, Mister Waiter . . . ," I said just as he was turning to walk away.

"Yes?"

I stood up so he would understand that the question I was asking was extremely important.

"Can you tell me if the famous restaurant reviewer Maria Cross is here yet?" I was so proud of my **professional** sound that I almost jumped out of my own skin when my parents both gasped.

"Frannie!" my mother shouted.

And my dad snapped, "Bird!"

The waiter and I looked at each other. We were both very confusified at my parents' reactions.

"What?" I asked.

"Remember what we explained to you?" my dad asked.

I shook my head no. My parents explained a **millionteen things** to me. How was I supposed to know the exact thing he was talking about?

My dad looked up at the waiter and said, "She's a little confused. She doesn't really know what she's saying."

The waiter **shrugged**, but had a curious look on his face, like he knew a special secret and was thinking about telling it to other people. I am very smart about **curious** looks and special secrets. After the waiter left, my parents turned back to me.

"First of all, we don't even know whether Maria Cross will be here tonight. She might very well have decided to come next Friday night. But, more importantly, restaurants aren't supposed to know the critics are at the restaurants, remember? So there should be no mention of her name, whatsoever," my dad reminded me.

I slapped my hand against my forehead. "I forgot about that!" I said. And while I did feel really bad about giving away a secret, I had to make a brain note about the word *whatsoever*. It was very grown-up and I wanted to use it as oftenly as possible.

CHAPTER

When the waiter came back, he had a bread basket and a pitcher of water with him. Just like the ones they had at **Spaghetti Lunch**! I looked up at him.

"Remember before how I asked about the famous restaurant reviewer, Maria Cross?" I could feel my parents getting ready to **slam** their hands against their foreheads.

"Yes . . . ," the waiter said, waiting for me to tell him a really **special** secret.

"Well, that was a mistake. I thought we were at a different restaurant where Maria Cross is supposed to be—"

"That'll be enough, Frannie," my dad interrupted.

"—but I was wrong about that because we're not at that restaurant. We're at this one. And she's not supposed to be here. Not tonight, or *whatsoever*. Maria Cross, I mean," I said.

For some reason that I did not understand, I could not **stop** talking. I could not stop explaining how Maria Cross wasn't going to be here. I just wanted to talk that expression off his face. The one that said *even though you are saying one thing I still believe the other thing you said earlier*.

And that is the reason why, when he came back to deliver our appetizers, I said, "So you believe me, right? About Maria Cross not being here?"

"Frannie!" my dad finally almost-yelled. I looked at him.

"What?" I asked as the waiter stood there waiting to hear what my dad was going to tell me.

"Enough."

When the waiter walked away, my table was very quiet except for the sound of **water-sipping and bread-chewing**. I looked over and saw him whispering to another waiter, and then I watched as that waiter went into the kitchen, and two minutes later a very sweaty, red-faced man dressed all in white came out and looked around the restaurant.

I knew exactly what they were doing. They were looking for Maria

Cross. My waiter had told! He hadn't **believed** me!

The waiters were looking and looking around until, **all of a sudden**, the big, sweaty man in all white nudged his chin in the direction of a lady, sitting all by herself. She was a very big lady, which made sense since her job was to eat. She had black, **curly** hair and she had something on her lap, which meant she was hiding something. Probably a pad of paper for notes. Even though I couldn't see exactly if I was right, I knew I was.

Maria Cross!

I nudged Elliott with my elbow and threw my eyeballs in her direction. When Elliott saw her, he didn't even have to ask who I was talking about. He knew. Sometimes he doesn't even have to read the thoughts in my brain. **Sometimes he can just hear them**.

I was going to do everything Maria Cross was going to do.

I looked up at my parents.

"Elliott and I are going to start our restaurant review now," I told them.

"Okay, just be quiet about it," my dad said.

"We will."

And then I opened my briefcase and pulled out my two pads and gave one to Elliott. I put mine **on my lap**, like Maria Cross, and Elliott did the same. Then we each held on to our pencils and waited. I knew we both looked very professional. Probably like we should have been in an **office**.

CHAPTER

The thing about restaurant reviews is that we did not know how to write them. We had never even read one before. We were **stumpified**.

Elliott was looking around the restaurant and I could see his brain trying to find words to **describe** everything. I stared at all the food, trying to think of words to describe salad. I looked down at what I had so far:

Salad.

I looked over and saw what Elliott had written down so far:

Crowded.

This was not a good sign. I looked over at Maria Cross. Then I looked at Elliott.

"We have to see what's on her pad," I told him.

Elliott nodded in agreement. Maria Cross would certainly have food descriptions on her pad that would **nevertheless** help us get started. That's when I got a geniusal idea.

"I have to go to the bathroom," I said.

"Me too," Elliott said.

"Go together and wait for each other, please," my mom said with her **face channel** turned to strict.

Maria Cross's table was on the

way to the bathroom. Elliott and I tried to get close so we could see her pad as we passed by. But we got too close because we banged right into her table! Her glass wobbled and she looked up from her lap and made a mad face at us. Suddenly I felt a hand on my shoulder. It belonged to my dad. He leaned over and said to Maria Cross, "I am so sorry about that."

"That's all right," she said in a really high kind of voice.

"You're supposed to be on your way to the bathroom," he said. "Please use it and come right back to our table. Is that understood?"

We said that we did understand and then we walked directly toward the bathroom. Right when we reached the bathroom area, my eyeballs got distractified. The kitchen was *right there*! And we could see exactly right inside it because there was no door!

There were a machillion people rushing around in there. Some people were yelling in another language and other people were cooking a millionteen things at once. There was a long table where waiters put plates with fancy food, and also bread baskets and pitchers of water!

Something on one of the plates looked a little weird. I took a couple steps closer. And that is when I saw the most newsbreaking story of ever.

I nudged Elliott and pointed toward a plate. When he saw the plate, he almost fainted. You will not in one hundredteen years believe what we saw in that kitchen on that plate.

BUGS!

My eyeballs were not even seeing things wrong. We stepped a little bit closer, and sure enough we saw the little **bug heads** popping out of their bug shells. Then a waiter came over and poured **warm butter** all over them, picked up the plate, and brought it out to serve it to someone!

"Should we tell someone?" I asked Elliott.

"I don't know," he answered.

"Someone is about to eat buttered bugs without even knowing it!"

Elliott just stood there with his eyes bulging out all over the place. He didn't know what to do, either.

We both stuck our heads **back in the kitchen** and nearly fell over when a couple of waiters came running out yelling, "Hot plates, very hot plates!"

"They seem very busy," Elliott said. He was right. I didn't want to interrupt them. So we went back to our table before my dad decided to **arrest us and put us in jail.**

Our main course had already been served. My parents seemed a little **angry** at us. Elliott and I sat down and I studied our plates for bugs.

"What in the world were you two thinking?" my mother asked as she cut into her chicken.

"We didn't mean to get so close to her table," I explained.

"It just sort of happened that way," Elliott added.

"You need to leave her alone and let her write her review, if that's even what she's doing," my mom said.

I looked at my mom's plate and then at my dad's to make sure there were no bugs on them. There weren't, but I was very **concerned** that someone in the restaurant *would* have bugs on their plate! That is

when I got the most fantastical idea.
I wrote something down on a piece
of notebook paper, ripped it out, and
handed it to Elliott.

Let's write a note to Maria
Cross and tell her about the bugs!

If anyone could stop people from
eating bugs, it was Maria Cross!
Elliott read my note and looked at me
with **a face** that said *Frannie—you
are a genius of the earth.*

I handed Elliott the pad because
he has very good handwriting. That
is why he is my **secretary**. Then I
whispered each sentence to him and he
wrote down every single word I said in
the very strictest letters. We know you
are here. We won't tell anyone. We saw
a waiter pour butter on a plate of insects
and then bring it out to a table. Someone

in this restaurant is now eating a dinner with bugs on their plate. It could be you!

When he was done, he showed it to me and I was very **impresstified** with the way it looked. He was very impresstified with how it sounded. Then I handed it back and he added:

Thank you,
The Secret People.

I gave him **the most gigantic smile** about that last line. Then I wondered how we were supposed to get this note to her.

"I have to go to the bathroom again," I told my parents.

Elliott looked confused.

"You just went," my dad said.

"I know, but I couldn't go. I need to try again," I said.

"Quickly, please," my dad said.

I got up and brought the pad with me. When I reached the bathroom, I tore the note off the pad of **paper** and folded it in half so no one could read it. Then I **tugged** on a waiter's sleeve and when he bent down I asked him if he would take the note to someone.

"Who?" he asked me.

I couldn't tell him her name because I wasn't supposed to let anyone know that Maria Cross, famous restaurant reviewer of the world, was here, so I had to point, which I felt bad about because **pointing is rude**.

"Her," I said, pointing to Maria Cross. The waiter nodded and took the note from me. Then, I actually *did* have to go to the bathroom.

The bathroom was very fancy. It

had music playing in it and an **actual waterfall** coming down a wall. There were a lot of different sprays on a shelf and I sprayed one just to see what it smelled like.

Roses!

The toilet didn't flush by itself like the usual toilets in restaurants did. Instead, this one had a flusher that hung down from the ceiling on a chain. It took me foreverteen minutes to figure out I was supposed to pull it in order to get it to **flush**.

When I went back to our table, I saw the waiter walk over to Maria Cross's table. I nudged Elliott and we both turned as she opened the note, read it, and then, at the top of her **lungs**, and I am not even making this up, she screamed, grabbed her purse and her coat, and ran out of the restaurant! Everyone stopped eating and watched her. When she got to the door, she **banged** into a lady and looked right in her face and yelled something that sounded like "Bugs!"

Then *that* lady shrieked, ran to her table, and whispered something in her husband's ear. They quickly got up and left, too.

And that is when things started to go not so right.

Suddenly, the customers in the front of the restaurant were **shrieking** and jumping up and yelling for their checks. The waiters and chefs were running out, trying to calm everyone down, but it didn't seem to work because before we even knew it, the front part of the restaurant was **nearly empty**.

My parents looked very confused. My dad turned to my mom. "What did she say?"

"I don't know," my mom answered. "Rugs?"

Then they looked at me and Elliott like we had **something** to do with it!

"What??" I asked them.

"Nothing," my mom said. "Just looking. Can't I just look at you?" she asked with an *I'm not really "just looking" at you, I'm suspicious that you are up to no good* face.

That felt like **a trick question**, so I looked at Elliott, who shrugged, and then I looked back at my parents and said, "I guess so." And then added, "But I don't have to like it one bit!"

CHAPTER

9

During the car ride home, my dad kept looking at us in the **rearview** mirror. His look asked if Elliott and I did something to make Maria Cross scream and run out of the restaurant. My mom turned around to face us.

"So you have no idea what Maria Cross, if that was even her, said when she ran out?"

Elliott and I shook our heads no. I felt **horrendimous** not telling them the truth, but I was a restaurant critic right now and we work in **secret**. My parents would have to learn about what happened once it was in the newspaper. Just like all the other readers in the world.

It was a really good thing that Elliott was sleeping over because we had to write this review as fast as possible. We had to get it in all the newspapers so the restaurant could get an **exterminator** and get rid of all

those bugs. Our parents were going to be so proud of us.

When we got home, Elliott and I rushed up to my desk and pulled two chairs together. He started to write about the restaurant (I told him about the bathroom so he wrote about that, too) and I wrote about the food. Then Elliott rewrote the whole review in his geniusal handwriting.

Tenley was going to babysit me and Elliott the next day. Since she knew about **healthy** things, we thought she should know about the bugs at Balloon. So our plan was to show her our review first.

Here is the review we wrote:

This is a restaurant review of the most awfulest restaurant in the world. It is written by two people: Frannie B.

Miller, who will review the food part, and Elliott Stephenson, who will review the restaurant part.

Tonight we had the most worst meal in the entire city of Chester. We had it at a new restaurant. The new restaurant is really bad first of all because it is called Balloon, but they forgot the letter n, so the awning just says Balloo. Also, it was VERY crowded. There were so many people there that we had to give our coats to someone to put away. But the worst, worst, worst thing is what we're about to tell you: It is not an opinion that there were actual insects in the kitchen and the waiter poured butter on them. Then he took that plate and brought it to someone who would eat BUGS in butter, without even knowing it! We wrote Maria Cross a note about this and she did the exact right thing and screamed and ran out of the restaurant!

Then lots of other people screamed and ran out of the restaurant. My parents did not hear what the people were screaming about and so we stayed all the way through to dessert. Then we left and came home to write this review. Thank you for reading this review. the end.

PS: There were some good things we forgot to tell you. The bathroom had a ceiling flusher that you pulled. Also there were sprays that smelled like roses and a waterfall that ran down a wall, which I did not see, but Frannie told me about.

CHAPTER 10

The next morning, we looked at the *Chester Times* because my parents have it **delivered** every day. We were relieved to see that Maria Cross did not write her review there yet. We wanted to be the first ones to review the terrible restaurant, Balloon. I had a very strong feeling in my **heart** that when the newspaper printers read it, they would hire me and Elliott as their new restaurant reviewers.

Tenley came over and said we were going to have a really fun day. Then we all walked into town so we could go to **the hobby store**. The hobby store is where we buy our hobbies. A for instance of what I mean is that sometimes Elliott and I like to tie-dye T-shirts. The hobby store is where we buy the tie-dye T-shirt kits.

On the walk over, we told her all about the bad restaurant and then handed her the **review**. She took the review from our very hands and read it right then and there. We watched her face grow very angrified.

"So the bugs were not crawling on the floor? They were on the plate?"

I nodded. "Yup. They were just right there, dead on a plate."

"In butter," Elliott added.

Tenley moved her face into a *gross* expression.

"You make it sound like there were a lot. It wasn't just one bug? Like a fly that **accidentally** flew onto the plate or something?"

"There were a lot of them. Like sixteen of them!"

"That is really revolting," Tenley said. *Revolting* was a really good word.

"It was *very* revolting," I said.

Tenley thought for a minute. Then she looked back at us and asked, "Are you one hundred percent positive that they were bugs? They couldn't have been anything else? Maybe a type of food that *looks* like bugs?"

"What kind of food looks like bugs?" I asked.

Tenley thought about this for a minute. "Caviar looks like hundreds of ants mushed together in a pile. Is that how they looked?"

I looked at Elliott and passed a brain note to him. It said, "She is not listening to us!" And Elliott sent one back that said, "I know, but I'm not the boss of her, so I can't really do anything about that!" I wondered whether I needed to use my English accent so she would really listen to me. But I decided against it.

"That is not how they looked because, like I just told you, there were about sixteen of them. And also, they were bugs!" I told her this with a face that did not move a muscle and that could only mean one thing: THEY WERE BUGS!

"They were *definitely* bugs," Elliott agreed.

"Well, if you're a hundred percent sure, then we have to do something right away," she said. Then she stared directly into my eyeballs. "Are you a hundred percent sure, Frannie?"

"A hundred percent," I said.

"And, Elliott," she asked looking directly into his eyeballs, "are you a hundred percent sure, too?"

"A hundred percent," he also said.

"Fine. Then we need to take action now," she said. "This is a very serious health issue."

I hadn't thought about that. It was true that we probably should have told people about the bugs instead of keeping them a secret.

"I have an idea," Tenley said, but

she didn't tell us the idea! She just walked really quickly, like we were late to meet her idea.

When we got to the hobby store, she finally told us what she was thinking.

"We are going to make signs." I thought this was a spectacular idea. We bought all the **supplies**. Then we sat at a table they had in the hobby store for making signs just like this. This is what we wrote in very big letters:

We made twelve hundredteen signs. Then we walked up and down the street taping our signs to poles, and **marched** right up to the restaurant, Balloon. It was closed because it was daytime, so we taped a sign to the front window.

We stood back and smiled at the good job we had done. When I looked down the street, I saw people already **crowding** around some of the signs and reading them. It was working!

Then, on our way home, we stopped at the **post office**, where Tenley bought us a stamp and an envelope. Tenley showed us how to look up the address for the *Chester Times* in the phone book at the post office. And then, because Elliott is my secretary and has geniusal handwriting, he addressed the letter:

Maria Cross's Boss
The Chester Times
345 Pearl Street
Chester, NY 10758

Elliott and I walked to the post office window and handed the window person our letter. I looked at her in a very strict but **polite** way and said, "It's very important that this go to the newspaper. Thank you very much."

Then she said, "I will personally see to it."

She was taking me very seriously. That felt really grown-up. Another thing that felt grown-up was her **name tag**. I am very interested in name tags. I made a brain note to make one for myself when I got home. Maybe I'd even wear it to school.

CHAPTER

11

When I got home, my parents were in the TV room watching the **boring** news of the world. Just as I was about to get too bored, I saw a newscaster standing in front of Balloon.

"This brand-new restaurant Balloo has a pest of a problem. According to signs, it seems Balloo is serving up more than food: It's serving bugs. Leslie Eisenberg was there last night, so we asked her to tell us what she saw."

Leslie Eisenberg's head filled up the screen. "I didn't see a thing. At some point, people just started screaming and half the restaurant ran out."

"That's certainly not a very good sign," the newscaster said. "I know I won't be making reservations there any time soon. Ed, back to you."

And that is when my parents turned off the **TV** and looked at each other.

"Bugs!" my dad shouted, slapping his hand down on his knee. Then he turned to my mom.

"Bugs?" she asked.

They both looked straight into my eyeballs.

"Birdy, did you see any bugs at Balloo?" asked my dad. It was time for me to tell them.

"Yes, as a matter of fact. I did. I

was the one to tell Maria Cross all about the bugs."

Their **expressions** turned serious.

"What exactly do you mean?" my mom asked.

I told them all about seeing the bugs on the plate, and writing the note to Maria Cross, and how she read it and then everyone **ran** out of the restaurant. And also about how we put up all the signs that made it on the actual **boring** news of the world! I

didn't even take **a breath** until I was finished speaking.

"What did these bugs look like, exactly?" my dad asked.

"They had little heads popping out of their shells."

And that's when I realized something. And that something was this: The bugs looked like snails. Slimy, slippy, disgusting snails.

And revolting. I don't know why my brain didn't think of this sooner. Sometimes it forgets things when it gets too full.

But you will not even believe this. Instead of being proud of me for saving everyone's lives, they got upset! And then, the **worst** news of the world came down into my ears. You are not even going to believe this either.

They *were* snails.

And, you are not going to believe your ears about this next news: At French restaurants, PEOPLE EAT SNAILS! The **fancy** name for it is *escargot*.

"But how could we know that grown-ups like eating snails?"

"How about asking?" my dad asked.

I squinched my face at that one.

Asking! Elliott and I hadn't even thought of that. We just went right ahead and **assumed**. Assuming is when you think you know something without asking. Mostly, I have started to learn that when I assume things, I am usually wrong.

"Let's just go back and put a sign on the restaurant saying we were wrong," I suggested.

And that is when both my parents started to get really **frantical**. My dad was worried about the signs being up. My mom was worried about the story being on the news. My dad was worried about Maria Cross. My mom was worried about the restaurant. I could not even believe that mistaking snails for bugs would cause all this **worry**!

CHAPTER

12

"I'll drive into town and take down the signs," my dad said as he grabbed his car keys off the **coffee table**. "And when I get back, I'm going to call Elliott's parents to make sure they speak to Tenley so that nothing like this happens again." My stomach dropped when I heard this. I hoped Elliott's parents wouldn't get too angrified with Tenley.

As my dad rushed out the door,

my mom rushed over to the computer. That's where she found out how to call the television station and also how to call Maria Cross! She called the news and told them the whole story. However and **nevertheless**, I had to call Maria Cross on my very own.

"How can I call her—I don't even know her?" I asked my mother.

I knew right away that I shouldn't have said this because of the way the breathing holes in my mother's nose got bigger and rounder.

"That certainly didn't stop you from sending her a note," my mother said in a talk-shout. "Now you have no choice but to deal with the consequences."

It is a scientific fact that I do not like to "deal with the consequences." Consequences are the bad things that happen to you after you've done a bad thing.

I was very nervous and frightened about talking to Maria Cross. Grown-ups can be scary sometimes. Especially the kind you've never even met before.

I took the phone into my bedroom and closed my door because I needed to be **all by myself** when I called her. Otherwise I would get too nervous.

I opened my music box and took out a couple of jelly beans. After I finished them, I felt **ready** to call. The phone rang. The phone rang again. The third time it rang, it only rang half because someone picked up.

"Hello?" a woman's voice said.

"Hi. May I please speak to Maria Cross, the very famous restaurant reviewer?" I asked.

That is when the lady **giggled** and said, "Well, who may I say is calling?"

"This is Frannie B. Miller of Chester, New York. I am actually and nevertheless a food critic myself and I have some very important information to give her."

"Is that so?"

"It really is," I said.

"Well, you're in luck," the lady said, "because you're talking to Maria Cross."

I gasped. "Wow," I said.

"Wow, indeed," she responded. *Indeed* is a very **wonderful** word that grown-ups use that I need to **remember**. "So what's this very important information you have for me?"

"I'm the one who sent you the note at Balloon saying that the restaurant had bugs in the kitchen, but  it turns out that they were not bugs at all. What they were, exactly, was SNAILS! My parents told me that adults eat snails! So

I need to tell you that I was wrong. There are no bugs at that Balloon restaurant."

"Actually," said Maria, "snails, like clams and squids, are mollusks, not insects."

That was a word I had never heard before. "They're mullets?" I asked.

This is when Maria Cross laughed really hard out loud. I would have laughed, too, but I didn't know what was so funny.

"Mullets are really bad haircuts," she explained, and that's when, instead of snails, I pictured a lot of bad haircuts on a plate and laughed out loud, too.

"About the note," she continued. "I'm afraid it wasn't me you gave it to."

I was stumpified. "It wasn't?"

"No, I haven't been to Balloo yet. I'm going next Friday night."

"Oh," I said. "Then who did I give the note to?"

"I don't know, but I'm sure you gave her quite a scare."

"I did. She ran out of the restaurant screaming."

This made Maria laugh right out loud again.

"You are quite a character, Frannie B. Miller," Maria Cross said. Then she asked, "What else did you say in your review?"

"Well, I said that there was a waterfall in the bathroom and there were sprays that smelled like roses. I also said that I didn't know why they left the *n* off the word *Balloon*."

Then she laughed really out loud.

"Frannie, you sound like a lot of fun."

"I am," I said. But then I worried that that sounded too **braggish**, so I added, "At least, sometimes."

"Say, would you like to be my dinner companion next Friday night at Balloo? You could help me write my review and I certainly would like to see the review you wrote."

I sucked in a fast **gulp** of happiness.

"Really?" I asked.

"Really," she said.

"Hang on and I'll go ask my mom."

Then I ran down the hall yelling in the most excitified way and she said **yes** and then I went back on the phone and I made grown-up plans with Maria Cross to review Balloon for the second time.

CHAPTER 13

My parents were still pretty angry
at me and had some conditions about
going back to Balloon. First, I had
to **apologize** to the actual owner of
Balloon before going back for another
meal. Plus, I had to think of a way to
show the owner I was sorry instead
of just *saying* I was sorry. That was a
really hard thing to figure out. THEN
I had to write to the "Dear Editors"
section in our local newspaper and

tell **the real story** AGAIN of what
happened. By the time I was done
with all those sorrys, I was going to be
foreverteen years old! At least I knew
for a scientific fact that I would never
ever do anything like this again!

I *also* had to be on my best behavior
with Maria Cross and not give away
the fact that she is **a reviewer**.

My parents decided they liked
Balloon so much that they made a
reservation for the same night, but
they would sit at a different table, of
course.

The really scary part was when I
had to go to Balloon and apologize.
We went on Thursday night. That
way, it would not have been **illegal**
for me to go back there the next day.

The owner was a very scary

French man. He did NOT think the story was funny at all. In fact, he was very serious and not only mad at me, but at my entire worldwide family. That gave me a very bad-day feeling in my **belly** because they didn't do anything wrong. He was red in the face and walked back and forth in front of us, throwing his hands **all over the place while he talked**. Finally, he ended by saying everything was okay, but . . .

"It was very embarrassing for us, you know."

I nodded my head because I did know.

I thought I knew how to make things better, actually, but I couldn't tell him because it was a secret. It had to do with Maria Cross. Which meant he was going to have to **wait**. But he was certainly going to be very surprised by that sorry. The other sorrys I could show him now. I turned around to my dad and he put the cookie jar filled with all the **jelly beans** in my hands. I turned around and handed them to the red French man.

"I won this at my school fair because I guessed almost the right number of jelly beans. My parents explained that I took something away from you by saying you had bugs when you didn't. That is why I decided that I would take something away from me and give it to you. Which is why I would like you to have all the jelly beans I've ever had in my entire worldwide life."

That is when the red French man

made a **teeny** little smile out of the corner of his mouth. I'm really smart about teeny little **corner** smiles. He took the jelly beans from me and said, "*Merci beaucoup*," which is how French people say "Thank you very much."

Then I turned around and my mom handed me the poster that I made for him to hang on the front door. It was a picture of me that I drew with a big **cartoon** bubble coming out of my mouth that said:

I am Frannie B. Miller and there are no bugs at balloon. What they are exactly are SNAILS! I made a mistake and I am very sorry.

When he saw the poster, the other corner of his mouth gave a teeny little smile, too. I was starting to feel **better about everything**. Even snails!

Then he looked at my parents and smiled at them and said, "*Je suis très impressionné!*"

That is how you say "I am very impressed!" in French.

CHAPTER 14

Since I apologized to the owner and he **accepted**, I was not afraid to go back to Balloon on Friday night. And you will never believe in your worldwide life what I'm about to tell you.

Maria Cross e-mailed my parents to say she was going to wear a disguise to Balloon! A for instance of what I mean is that when famous restaurant critics go to restaurants they sometimes wear

wigs and glasses and hats so no one recognizes them! The best part of it was that she said I could wear one, too!

I wore my **prettiest dress**, the blue one with the yellow flowers all over it. That part was not my disguise. But my dad's **old glasses** with the lenses taken out *were* part of my disguise. So were the **millionteen barrettes** in my hair. Also, I brought my briefcase: business cards, résumé, envelopes, pencils, and a broken remote control so the briefcase would feel heavy.

When we got to the restaurant, we saw a woman waiting outside. She was very tall with black hair that went past her chin and glasses. Her glasses were just like mine except they still had lenses in them! She didn't look anything like the wrong Maria Cross.

But I wanted to know what she looked like without the disguise.

"Maria, if that's a wig, then what's your real hair like?" I asked.

"Frannie!" my mother shouted. "That's not a very polite question!"

Maria laughed. "It's okay."

I was glad Maria said it was okay for me to ask. Because I really wanted to know.

"My hair is long and blond. And the glasses are fake, if you're wondering."

Once we were inside, my parents went to their own table and I sat down with Maria Cross. She asked me all sorts of questions, like: *Tell me more about yourself!* and *Would you like to order off the adult menu tonight?*

I did order off the adult menu. It was **the most fantastical dinner**

I've ever had. Not the food so much, but every other part. Maria gave me a piece of paper from her pad and I got to write down all the words that came to my mind about the food. Then she explained the way she tasted food, and it was very interesting, but my tongue didn't taste anything *silky* or *tender*. It just tasted like carrot soup and boring old chicken.

The surprise of the night was that Maria ordered escargot! When they arrived they looked as **buggy** as they did before. I could not believe my worldwide eyes that she ate them. Then I could not even believe my eyes even more when she liked them.

"Part of a food critic's job is to try new things. How about you try a snail?" she asked, pushing the plate toward me. My stomach was very worried, but like I said earlier, I'm a very jobbish kind of person. If trying new things is part of the job, then I will **try new things**. She showed me the way to pull the snail out of its shell with a very **skinny** fork. Then I closed my eyes and held my nose from the inside and put the snail in my actual mouth! And then I chewed and you will not even believe this scientific fact: I liked it! Maria Cross was very proud of me for being so brave. I was proud of me, too. And, also, really surprised that my mouth liked the **snail taste**.

Then, at the best part—dessert— Maria Cross asked my parents to join us. You will not even believe it about the desserts. We ordered about **three hundred desserts** to share. The best was the slice of chocolate cake, which was as thick as eighty slices put together. And there was chocolate mousse inside of it! And inside of that? STRAWBERRIES! It was the best dessert I've ever had in my entire life as a person.

Then Maria Cross told me the most exciting things about restaurant reviews. You got to give out stars. Five stars is the very best and zero stars is the very worst. She asked how many stars I would give Balloon and I told her I'd give it five. My new review would say that this restaurant was **spectacular**. Telling her how good I thought the restaurant was was my other way of showing my sorry.

At the end of the meal, we walked her to her car, and that was when she handed me something. It was a small piece of paper and I looked at it. It had her **name and number** on it. It was her **business card**! I was so excitified, and that is when I remembered I had business cards, too! I opened my briefcase and took out a business card and handed it to Maria Cross. She put it right in her purse so it would never get lost.

"Don't forget to look at Wednesday's paper," she said as she got in her car. "You might find yourself in it!" And then she waved and drove away.

That night I got home and wrote my second review of the restaurant Balloo. I decided to leave the *n* off the name because Balloo is what the chef calls it and it's his restaurant. I wondered if Maria Cross said the same things in her review as I said in mine.

I could not wait to find out what she said. I also could not believe what a good restaurant reviewer I was turning out to be.

Maybe one day I'd even open my own restaurant. Elliott could stand in the front where people would give him their names and I could be the main waitress. Maria Cross could eat there for free. I'd invite Mrs. Pellington and I wouldn't drop one thing on her. I'd even let the red French man work there, if he wanted. My mom and dad would have a regular table like we have in the dining room at home. It would be the coziest, best restaurant ever. I already have a name for it: Balloon. And you know what will be the special of the night? Snails.

Balloo

by Maria Cross

4 and a half stars

Smack in the center of Chester, NY, sits a brand-new French restaurant whose younger patrons are confused by the missing *n* at the end of its name. Outside of that missing *n*, there's not much missing at Balloo. The toasted almond and beet salad was exquisite. The pairing of salt and sweet hit just the right notes. The Rosemary Chicken was silky and tender and the Chocolate Mousse Cake with strawberries was the best I've ever had. The snails caused early alarm. Mistaken for insects by a budding young food critic, these snails even made it on the news. And well they should. They are newsworthy snails: the stand-out in a sea of stand-outs. I'd travel far to dine on Balloo's snails. And so should you. They are divine.

Balloo
by Frannie B. Miller
Grown-ups eat weird things like seaweed and snails and probably other things that come

from the bottom of the ocean
that I don't want to know
about. Last week I didn't know
that you could eat snails, but
now I do. That's because I
told the entire world of Chester,
New York, that Balloo, the new
restaurant with no n on the
end of its name, was serving
bugs. Really, they were snails
and I was wrong. That is a
for instance of why you should
eat at Balloo without worrying.
And also because I even ate
one and it tasted good. Not as
good as the desserts, though.
The desserts are delicious and
there is nothing weird in them.
Thank you for reading this.

THE END.